Bonded For Life

Written By:
Tesa Erven

PUBLISHING

ISBN13: 978-1540527837
ISBN 10: 1540527832

Cover: Miss Web Designer LLC

Weeping may endure for a night

but joy comes in the morning.

Psalm 30:5

ACKNOWLEDGEMENTS

To my Heavenly Father: Thank you for your grace, mercy, and all the many blessings.

To my mom Tess and my dad Glen: With all my love, thank you for all that you do.

To my children Teric and Tierra: I love you so very much. Follow your dreams and don't give up.

To my husband Bruce: You are my love, my world. Thank you for having my back always.

To my Family, Extended Family, and Friends: Special shout out to Sheila, Dandre, Doreen, Grandma O., Helen, Phyllis, Diane, and Jennifer. Thank you for your love and support. I miss you my angel, Grandma T.

To my bestie Ashaki and her family: Glad to have you on this journey with me.

To my Cali Family: How can we forget the house on the hill (lol) Natalie, Troy, Gloria, Ebony, and Bernard. Miss you all so much! Special book dedication to the ones who started it all, R.I.P. Kitt, Yolanda, and Cali love.

To my NJ Family: Eric, Bessie, Chaun, Shirley, Eric E., Jody, Shay, Takeoversalon Tammy, Meredith, Curt, Ernest (andortoys.com), Toria (ShaTor), Coco, Kathy, Martha, Mike, Antoinette, Dion, James, Velandrea, and Ms. Mary.

To my LHH Family: Joann, Ama, Linda, Joe L, Raoul, John, Art, Bob R., and Safiya. You are all the best!

To my Author Family: Sharona Seigler (J. Asmara) at EP Publishing, LaShaunda Hoffman (SORMAG), Paulette Nunlee (5Star Proofing), Shauna-Kay Battick (Humbird Multimedia Designer), Ella D. Curry (EDC Creations), Papaya Wagstaff-Speight (Promoter), Sharon Blount, Cedric Lewis, LaToya Murchison, Ann Marie Johnson-Bryan, Kisha Green-Frazier, Desiree A. Cox, Chelle Ramsey, Suzette Harrison, Kaywanda Lamb, Annie Johnson, Quashon Davis, W. Parks Brigham, and Rashonda Jones-Aiken. You are an amazingly talented group of people that I admire and appreciate having you in my life. Thank you for pushing me forward. I wish you all much success.

To my Readers: Thank you for escaping into my world and giving my books a chance. You know what I say, "If you like it, tell a friend. If you don't, keep it to yourself and pray for me."

Hugs, T

Table of Contents

The Aftermath of

LOVE CHANGES EVERYTHING

"I can't believe that just happened," Bradsen said to himself as he pulled his car out from in front of his twin brother, Jacksen, and his wife, Cynthia's house. He glanced over at Renee who had a stunned expression on her face.

With a concerned tone he asked, "Are you okay?" He watched as the glistening tears in her oval-shaped eyes threatened to spill over.

Renee's voice quivered as she replied, "I'm fine. Although, it's not every day I have a drink thrown in my face."

Sabrina, Renee's best friend and former roommate, chimed in from the backseat, "I can't believe she did that. There was way too

1

much tension in there."

Renee lowered her head. "Yeah there was. But, Brenda has every right to be angry with me. I was knowingly having an affair with her husband. I'm glad she was able to release some of her anger. It could have been worse, you know. She could have pulled out a gun and shot me," Renee added, attempting to make light of the situation.

"That's not funny, Renee." Bradsen glared at her. "Okay, you cheated with her husband. I get it. But, I thought we were past it. Apparently not."

"Let's face it. It was too soon. I had a feeling we shouldn't have gone there tonight."

"Yep," Sabrina said.

Derrick joined the conversation. "I agree."

Renee cleared her throat and laughed at them. "Really now? So, earlier when we were in the car contemplating on whether or not we should go into the house, no one bothered to say, 'Oh, there's a small possibility that you may get your butt kicked.' You guys are unbelievable."

"A drink thrown in your face. But your butt kicked? That wouldn't have happened. At least, not with me standing there," Sabrina assured her.

Bradsen hadn't said much. Renee looked over at him and noticed tension on his handsome face. "Are you alright?"

Bradsen looked at her and softly uttered, "We'll talk about it later."

Silence filled the car until Derrick asked, "You two still coming to my game, right?" The six three, well-built rookie linebacker would be starting in his first game on Sunday. Sabrina nudged him in the side. "What?" Derrick mouthed.

"Yes, we'll be there," Bradsen said as he pulled into Renee's apartment complex. Once they said their goodbyes, Sabrina and Derrick headed to his car and Bradsen and Renee went into her place.

"Now do you want to tell me what's wrong?" Renee asked when Bradsen closed the door.

"Baby, I'm so sorry about tonight. I feel terrible. I should have never pressured you into going. Me and Jacksen kind of thought enough time had passed. I really wish there was a way we could all get along."

Renee put her arms around his waist and leaned back to look up into his brown eyes and clean-shaven, dark brown face. Bradsen stood a couple inches over six feet, easily towering over her five-and-a-half feet.

"I don't know what you want me to do, Bradsen. This is tough. I didn't expect your family to accept me with open arms. I chose to be the other woman. It was a bad decision on my part, but I have to live with the choices that I've made, not you. I love you, but I don't want you to be miserable because you can't have it both ways. There's always going to be some kind of animosity towards me from your family."

"Baby, I realize this is hard and I love you too, but there has to be a better way-" He stopped mid-sentence.

Renee pulled her arms from underneath his. She spat, "A better way to what? To us trying to get together again. It's not going to happen. I'm sorry to tell you that I'm not welcomed there, and if that's a problem for you then I guess you could-"

Bradsen cut her off, "Don't you dare say it, Renee. I'm not going anywhere. You are the one I want, and we'll have to figure out something, because I won't give up on us."

Renee shook her head while Bradsen pulled her back into his embrace. With her petite frame wrapped in his arms, she always felt safe with him. He wanted to reaffirm his love for her to show her that they would get through it no matter what happened. But he knew only time would tell.

THE MEETING PLACE

It was another Saturday night at Club Dread. Sonya St. Jermaine sat at the bar and finished what should've been her last sour apple martini for the night. She glanced at her watch and figured that she would be able to handle one more before the club closed. Getting the bartender's attention and placing her order, she turned in her chair and checked the dance floor. Normally she would have been on the floor the majority of the night, but that night she wasn't in the mood for dancing. However, she did sway her body to the beat once she got her drink.

"Hey beautiful," a male voice called out

from behind her. "Why aren't you dancing tonight?"

Sonya spun around to answer and was pleasantly surprised to find the club's deejay standing there. She hadn't noticed him walk to the bar from the booth. Sonya politely smiled and said, "I don't know. I'm not really feeling it, I guess." She shrugged her shoulders.

He playfully placed his hand on her forehead. "Are you feeling okay?"

"I'm fine." She pushed his hand away.

"I'm just checking because you are here when the door opens and closes and out there dancing," he joked. "What is it about Club Dread you like so much?"

Sonya took another sip of her martini, deciding on whether to dismiss or entertain his question. As long as she had been going there, she'd noticed him sometimes watching her, but they'd barely exchanged two words.

She wondered, what made him speak to her on that particular night.

"I guess we have something in common."

He raised a brow and asked, "What could that be?"

Sonya chuckled. There was only one word to describe her faithful drive to Club Dread on Saturday nights, it was loyalty. "We're both loyal to Club Dread."

Yusef didn't have long to talk before the song ended, but he still took a second and sat at the available seat next to hers.

"For as long as you've been loyal here, why haven't you told me your name?" Yusef asked. Although he knew who she was from Channel Five News, they hadn't formally met.

Sonya smirked at him and said, "You've never asked so I've never told you," with a slight roll of the neck.

Yusef held his mouth open in surprise,

"Oh, so it's like that!"

"No, I'm only kidding. My name is Sonya St. Jermaine," Sonya stated as she extended her hand to his.

"I'm Yusef Turner and it's finally nice to place a name with the pretty face."

Sonya gave him a soft smile.

"I better get back before the song ends and people start to complain about the deejay. Would it be possible if we could finish this conversation later, perhaps after the club?"

Sonya said "Yes" before she knew it. The alcohol had a lot to do with her saying yes because she wasn't in the least bit attracted to Yusef. He wasn't ugly. It was just that his six-foot frame, light brown skin, and husky build wasn't her type. However, after the day she had, she'd do just about anything to spice up her evening; especially if it meant not going home alone.

* * *

Yusef continued to watch Sonya throughout the night. For someone that wasn't enjoying the club, she appeared to be having a good time from what Yusef observed. He thanked the crowd for coming out while the last song played. He watched as Sonya exchanged a few words with a man who had whispered something in her ear. Why was he watching? She had already agreed to wait for him.

Sonya made her way over to the deejay booth. "I'll meet you in the parking lot," she quietly said to Yusef. "I know you have to pack up your equipment, so take your time."

Before he could protest, Sonya headed out the door with the man she had been talking to. The only reassurance he had that she wouldn't leave was when she glanced back at him and smiled. Relaxed now, Yusef would finally get the chance to find out about the

11

mysterious woman who frequented the bar on Saturday nights.

* * *

"So Ms. St. Jermaine, tell me a little something about you?" Yusef asked from the passenger seat of Sonya's car while they were parked in front of the nightclub.

She sat behind the steering wheel and thought, *why is he asking me this question? It's three o'clock in the morning and I'm sure he cares less about the specifics of my life, or could he really be interested?* Sonya didn't like volunteering information about herself, especially to a guy she'd just met. However, there was something about Yusef that intrigued her. He wasn't the finest brother, but there was this certain charisma that he possessed. Maybe it was seeing him once a week that made her feel comfortable with talking to him.

"I'm twenty-eight, single, and live alone in

San Francisco in a two-bedroom condo. And I don't have any kids."

"Wow, you're straight to the point!" Yusef hadn't expected Sonya to come on so strong. However, he got the hint, "Am I coming with you?"

Sonya leaned over to the passenger side and kissed him gently with the gorgeous red lips he'd admired all night. She whispered softly in his ear and said, "Get in your car and follow me."

* * *

Driving the thirty minutes from Oakland to San Francisco definitely had Yusef uncomfortable. It wasn't the idea of going to Sonya's place, rather the early morning drive to get there after a few beers, the adrenaline of playing music all night, and the fact that he had been up all day. He was relieved when she pulled her car into the garage and directed him to park in the visitor's spot.

13

Sonya lived in a ritzy development known as the Gateway in the Financial District. It was considered prime real estate for young professionals that worked close to downtown. It was ideal for Sonya because she wanted to be near her job.

"This is a nice area," Yusef commented when he entered into the condo. "I didn't even know these condos were here." He admired the view from her living room and took in the sights of the Bay Bridge and its lights that glowed in the distance. "How long have you been living here?"

"About two years now and I really like it here. The neighborhood is quiet and I've always liked living on a dead-end street. Less traffic."

"I see black is your favorite color." Yusef's eyes scanned her plush black suede sofa and dining room table with the matching suede chairs.

"Yes, I'm very basic and like my space as well as my privacy. That's why you don't see much furniture."

Yusef surveyed the rest of the living room and found an entertainment center that held a fifty-two inch television, countless DVDs, and music CDs. There was no coffee table, no paintings hanging on the walls, and no family photos lying around.

"Are you sure you live here?" He couldn't believe her condo had so much space that she wasn't making use of. Although, everything was nice and tidy, you wouldn't see her home showcased on the HGTV channel.

"Let's go upstairs and find out." Sonya took Yusef by the hand and led him up the stairs. They passed the spare bedroom that was just as dull as the living room before they made it to her room. He was glad to see that the master bedroom had at least picked up in taste with a king-sized poster board bed that was outlined in a black, white, and red decorative setting.

Sonya guided him to the bed and immediately pushed Yusef down on the bed and undressed him. She unzipped his pants and pulled off his charcoal gray slacks along with his boxers. Sonya was happy with him because he was already aroused and anticipated the moment that he would be inside of her. With the nine or so inches he'd shown, there was no doubt in Sonya's mind that he would be able to penetrate a deep thrust against her.

They were both tired but that wouldn't stop them from pleasuring each other. Sonya quickly removed her designer red form-fitting dress, along with a red wispy bra and matching thong. Yusef's eyes clearly indicated he was pleased with what she had revealed. Excited, he hurriedly unbuttoned his light gray shirt exposing a slightly hairy chest. Sonya moved to him and placed light kisses on his stomach circling around his belly button. He massaged her shoulders and caressed her neck with his soft full lips. Yusef inhaled deeply, enjoying every touch, not knowing where their sexual act would take them emotionally. But, he wasn't concerned because all he knew was that he wanted her that night. Yusef slid his properly protected manhood inside of her and let their bodies flow to the rhythm of his motion until they both passed out from exhaustion.

A few hours later, Yusef shook Sonya awake. "Sonya, I have to go."

Sonya glanced over at the digital clock on her dresser that read: 6:55 a.m. *Why so early?* She was too tired to think about it.

"Okay, I'll walk you out."

Sonya reached for her robe that was at the foot of the bed and stumbled down the stairs.

"Thank you, Sonya. I had a really nice

time and would like to see you again if that's possible?"

"I'll be back at the club next week and I'll see you then."

"I was hoping to see you away from the club."

"Let's talk about it later, Yusef. Right now, I just want some sleep."

They said their goodbyes and Sonya ran up the stairs and climbed back into bed. She only had a few hours to rest before it was time to go to her brother Derrick's first NFL game.

* * *

"Where were you all night?" Those were the words Yusef was greeted with when he entered his house.

"Hello to you, too," he muttered to the woman who stood in front of him, blocking the entryway to the bedroom.

Donna Warren was well aware of the

nightlife of a deejay. There was the non-stop partying and the constant flirtatious behavior from various females that would request a song and then dance seductively right in front of the booth. She trusted Yusef because he never gave her any reason not to. If he wasn't coming home, he always called to let her know that he was okay. Usually it was just that he was too tired to drive, or he was staying at a friend's house. However, the night before wasn't the case. He had forgotten to call. That put doubt in her mind that maybe he was somewhere he shouldn't have been.

Yusef saw the disappointment in her eyes, but he didn't feel up to arguing any more than Donna wanted to. She wanted answers, but he didn't give any and she didn't attempt to force him to. Yusef had never cheated on Donna until Sonya. He couldn't understand what it was about Sonya that made him forget why he shouldn't have followed her home in the first place. He snapped out of his thoughts when Donna pushed past him when he didn't answer.

Although Donna and her daughter, Katina, spent the majority of their time at Yusef's place, they weren't officially living together. She still had her apartment that she would go to periodically. That moment was one when Donna was grateful she still had her own apartment and that Katina still stayed with her dad on the weekends.

"There's breakfast for you on the table. I'm going home." Donna grumbled and slammed the door on her way out, leaving Yusef alone with his thoughts.

GAME TIME

There was a clear blue sky on that Sunday afternoon-a great day for football. Derrick St. Jermaine took a deep breath while he stood in the tunnel. He looked up into the crowd at Levi Stadium that held about sixty-five thousand people. There were tons of screaming fans which included his own cheering squad of his parents, Sonya, Sabrina, Renee, and Bradsen. It was his time to shine and he was ready for the first game of the season. He had a lot of anxiety and great expectations. The moment felt surreal when his name and number were finally called by the announcer, "Number Fifty-

Eight, Derrick St. Jermaine, starting outside linebacker." The crowd went wild as he ran out onto the field for the first time.

For a rookie, Derrick had a great game. His efforts, led the way for the San Francisco Forty-Niners' first win of the season. Coming out from the locker room, the media was in a frenzy trying to get Derrick's attention. There were cameras and reporters everywhere, but when Derrick saw his parents, sister, and girlfriend, he went to talk to them first.

"Hey guys," he said, pumped up. "How did I do?"

He smiled while they cheered for him. His parents spoke at the same time. "Oh son, you did great" and "We're so proud of you" as they each hugged him.

"Hey, brother dear," Sonya called out using the pet name she had given him. "You think you're all that, huh?" she joked. "Great game, but don't forget about the media. They are your eyes and ears now, too."

"I won't, just let me sneak a quick kiss to my girl."

"Hey, baby." Derrick hugged Sabrina and then kissed her lips.

"Hey, superstar, you were in your zone. Congratulations, sweetheart." Sabrina kissed him again.

"Thanks baby. Where's Renee and Bradsen? I thought they were coming."

"Renee and Bradsen had another commitment and had to leave right after the game."

"Oh, okay."

"Excuse me, Derrick," Megan Richards from Channel Five's Sports Edition interrupted them. "Can we have a few minutes of your time?"

"Sure." He turned to Sabrina, gave her another kiss, and said, "I'll be back, beautiful."

Before Derrick went with Megan, Sonya quickly grabbed his arm. "Watch out for that one," she warned him softly.

"Hi Sonya," Megan said as she waved hello. "Why didn't you tell me your brother was big time?" Megan pulled Derrick away, as they walked off, before Sonya had a chance to reply.

Megan Richards was the main sports reporter for Channel Five News. At twenty-six, she was an aggressive go-getter that didn't take no for an answer. Standing about five eight with baby blue eyes, her blond flowing hair and a perfectly shaped body matched her gorgeous face. She was dressed to impress in a designer outfit that perfectly hugged her curves. Sabrina peered at Megan with a nasty look on her face. Sonya mumbled to her, "Don't worry, sis, I don't like her either."

"So Derrick St. Jermaine, how did you

feel about your first football game? Tell us about all the emotions and what was going through your mind when you first came out?" Megan asked, offering him the microphone.

"Man, I'm just speechless about this moment." Derrick beamed. "I'm so excited and it felt good to be out there on the field to show what I can do. It was a great game and everybody played well. Everybody contributed their best and I'm just glad we were able to get this win. I'm ready to see where the team can go from here."

"Thanks Derrick. We look forward to seeing you out there. Good luck with the season. I'll be watching." Megan quickly winked at him.

Derrick caught the undertone in her statement, but brushed it off. He then went on to finish the rest of the interviews from other media outlets before calling it a day.

* * *

Sonya was still tired from her previous night with Yusef, so she laid across her bed after Derrick's game. She rolled on her side to find her cell phone so she could call her sorority sister, Brenda Hawkins, to see what happened the night before. She'd heard from Derrick that dinner hadn't gone quite as planned. Sonya knew it would be disastrous and couldn't understand why they all wanted to hang out together. It didn't make any sense to her. It was bad enough she, herself, had to be cordial with Renee for the sake of her brother and Sabrina's relationship.

"Hey, Brenda," Sonya said when Brenda answered the phone.

"Hey girl. What's up?"

"I heard you lost your cool last night."

Brenda chuckled. "I tried to hang in there, Sonya, and was good until the end of the night. I started to think about the two of them together when everyone was laughing and having a good time. The next thing I know, my drink went flying out of my hand."

"Wow, I would have loved to be a fly on the wall."

"Yeah and as quickly as it happened, everyone got out of there, too. You would have thought the house was on fire." Brenda laughed at the memory.

Sonya joined her laughter. "What did Kayron say?"

"Not much. He didn't seem too surprised by my actions, so he may have mentally prepared himself for whatever happened."

"That's crazy."

Brenda quickly changed the subject. "So how was the club? I know how much you love that place, so what did I miss?"

"Now you know I don't kiss and tell," Sonya replied playfully. "If you missed it, then you missed it. But, in this case I can't keep it to myself. Guess who I hooked up with last night?"

"I don't know." Brenda tried to think. When no one came to mind, she said, "It was probably Dray and his no-good ass."

Sonya sucked her teeth. Dray McKinnis was definitely at the club and although Sonya went outside with him, they hadn't hooked up in a while. Sonya and Dray had a very complex relationship. One week, they were spending quality time together. Then the next, they couldn't stand the sight of each other. With the exception of sex, it just didn't work out for them to be a couple.

Dray was what one would call a player, because his God's gift to women mentality gave him that reputation. He had the look, the charm, and the right amount of roughness, thanks in part to his profession as an Oakland firefighter. Dray was five-eleven, a light shade of brown and had thick well-defined muscles. A smooth bald head and a goatee completed his look. He was sexy-but trouble.

Sonya thought back to the night she'd met Dray at the club.

He strolled over to the bar to order a drink when he spoke to Brenda. They knew each other from living in the same neighborhood. As he gazed at Sonya's familiar face with those dark slanted eyes of his, in a deep voice, he had asked her why his favorite news reporter wasn't dancing. Sonya had instantly blushed. It warmed her heart when people recognized her from Channel Five News. At the time, her response was short and direct: she didn't feel like dancing. Dray pondered on what to say next because he couldn't offer to buy her a drink; her glass was already full. They continued with small talk and by the end of the night, she had followed him home and that was the beginning of many nights to come.

Snapping out of her thoughts, Sonya said, "I hooked up with Yusef."

"Who is Yusef?" Brenda hadn't heard that name mentioned before.

"He's the deejay from Club Dread."

"Really?" Brenda blurted out. "That's different."

"Yeah. He's not my usual type, but he has nine inches of pure beauty."

"Sonya, how many?" Brenda repeated jokingly.

"Nine, maybe even nine and a half. All I know is he was far deep inside of me." Sonya shivered at the thought.

"So I take it that it was good."

"It was better than good."

"Are you going to see him again? Seeing as he's not really your style."

"Of course, I'm going to see him again. I'm not going to stop going to the club."

"You know what I mean," Brenda yelled into the phone.

Sonya and Yusef hadn't discussed much before or after the sex, but she had assumed he was in a relationship when he up and left before seven o'clock that morning.

"I guess so. We hadn't really talked about it."

"Don't assume anything. Especially, if you two didn't talk about it," Brenda replied. "Sonya, I have to go. Are you coming this way next week?"

"You know I am."

"Okay, I'll see you then."

Sonya hung up the phone and thought about Brenda's statement about not assuming. She had made a valid point; however it didn't matter as she wouldn't dare involve herself with Yusef because he simply wasn't her type.

* * *

Derrick and Sabrina made it home after having dinner in celebration of his first game. Sabrina went into their master suite to run a hot bath for Derrick, because he was a little sore. She lit some aromatic candles on both sides of the whirlpool tub and then added essential oils to the water. She turned on R&B slow jams that played through the built-in speakers that surrounded the room. As she checked the water temperature, the already naked Derrick snuck up behind her and said, "Why don't you join me?"

Sabrina turned to face the lovely sight of him, taking in every inch of his athletically-toned body. "Baby, this is for you. I know you must be aching, so how about I wash your back?"

"How about I wash yours?" Derrick asked as he kissed her on the neck, aware she couldn't resist him when he kissed her there.

Her breathing became rapid. "Baby."

He pulled her body closer to his. "Come on, take off your clothes and join me."

Sabrina melted in Derrick's strong arms, and once they broke apart, she slid off her clothes and stepped into the water.

The jets were flowing and the steam from the heated water had their bodies feeling good. Derrick pulled her close to him and kissed her some more. He started with gentle kisses that intensified with passion, and then he rubbed soap all over her as his hands roamed her body. Sabrina returned the favor by lathering his body. She deep-massaged his lower back and thighs before she moved to his penis and slowly stroked him. Derrick got lost in her rhythm, and began to swell in her hands.

"Ummmm, baby, that feels good. I want you so bad."

"Oh, you do?" Sabrina teased as she sped up her tempo.

"Oh baby," Derrick said as he pulsated in her hand. "Don't do me like this. I got to feel you."

"Hmmm...ask me nicely," she said as she outlined the tip of the head.

"Oh baby, *please* let me feel you."

"Since you asked so nicely, I guess I can make that happen," she teased.

Derrick pulled her close to him. He sucked her breasts while she closed her eyes and enjoyed the feel of his mouth on her. Derrick pulled her on top of him and pushed his way slightly into her. Sabrina let out a sound of pleasure as he filled her walls. Their bodies moved as one as they splashed around in the tub. Derrick gave Sabrina two good orgasms before leaving the tub, drying them off, and heading over to the bed. They danced around the California king-sized bed until they were both sexually satisfied.

As Sabrina showered, Derrick laid across

the bed, thinking, as he basked in the aftermath of their lovemaking. He had fulfilled his game obligations that day, but he knew as much as he loved Sabrina, they still needed to talk. He wanted to know how she really felt about the day's events. It was only the first game and the women had already started to flock to him. He knew the more media attention he got, the more reactions he would receive from other women. He wanted to make sure Sabrina would be okay.

"Baby, can we talk?" he asked Sabrina when she came back into the bedroom.

"Of course. About what?"

"How are you feeling about everything that's going on so far?"

"Really Derrick? I feel good. I love being here with you."

"You mean the world to me, Bri. I don't want anything to come between us, despite efforts from outside sources."

"Do you think that would happen?"

"It's possible if we don't keep the lines of communication open," Derrick replied.

"I know it's going to get a little rough with the female appreciation of you that will soon follow, but I'm here for you. And as long as you continue to show me the same respect as I give you, we will be fine."

Derrick smiled. "I love you, Bri."

Sabrina returned his smile and jokingly said, "I love you too, Derrick, but don't test me.

"Baby, you know that won't happen," he reassured her as he pulled her back down into his arms." They both laid in comfortable silence before falling asleep.

STAY OR WALK AWAY

Megan Richards purposely made her way to stand by the men's locker room after practice ended. She wanted to be noticed, but not by just anyone. Megan wanted to be seen by Derrick; she was mesmerized by his looks and charismatic charm. Everything about Derrick turned her on. Definitely interested in him, she knew he had a girlfriend but that wouldn't deter her from getting what she wanted. Derrick walked out the locker room and immediately saw Megan.

"Hey, it's you again," Derrick said as she approached him. "What brings you here, Ms. Richards?"

"I told you I would be watching, and please call me Megan."

37

"Um...okay Megan. Do you like what you've seen so far?"

Megan blushed. "It depends on what *you're* showing me. Where's your girlfriend?"

"Why do you ask?"

"I thought maybe you had a few minutes to talk, tell me more about you."

Derrick looked at the time. Just as he was about to respond, his cell phone rang. By the ringtone, he knew it was Sonya.

"Excuse me," he said as he answered it. "Hey sis. What's up?"

Megan frowned.

"Hey, brother dear," Sonya greeted him on the other end. "What are you up to?"

"Nothing, I'm about to leave practice."

"Do you have time to grab a bite to eat?"

"Sure. Where do you want to meet?"

"How about Kincaid's in Oakland? I could go for their maple grilled chicken salad."

"Sounds good. I'll see you in an hour."

"Okay. See you then."

"Sorry, Ms. Richards, *I mean Megan,* but I have to go."

"Maybe some other time."

"Yeah, maybe." Derrick turned and walked away.

* * *

Kincaid's was a popular eatery known for its prime steaks, fresh fish, and a variety of seafood. Located on the waterfront at Jack London Square, the restaurant had beautiful views of the marina. Sonya arrived early and picked a table in front of the large bay windows that overlooked the water. She watched the passing sailboats until Derrick arrived.

"Hey, sis." Derrick greeted her with a hug as he joined her at the table. "As usual, you're looking good, rocking those blue dots."

All day Sonya had received compliments on her stylish designer outfit, sporting a royal blue polka dot blouse and black slacks. Her shoulder length hair was side swept up into a twist style. Heads had turned in admiration as she'd entered the restaurant.

"Blue dots?" She laughed. "Thanks. How was practice?"

"Good. I ran into your girl afterwards," he joked.

The waiter interrupted to take their orders of Sonya's favorite maple grilled chicken salad and a huge porterhouse steak with all the trimmings for Derrick. They could tell he recognized Derrick as the waiter praised his play on Sunday. Sonya shooed him away, eager to get back to their conversation.

"Okay, so where were we? My girl?" Sonya asked, confused.

"Yeah, Megan Richards from Sports Edition. She was waiting there to talk to me."

Sonya shook her head. "Derrick, can't you

tell by now that she wants you and not just for an interview?"

She studied his face and her tone turned serious. "I like Sabrina for you and would hate for you to mess up your relationship with her, all because some other woman shows some interest in you."

Derrick listened before saying, "I know, sis. I actually had this same conversation with Sabrina. Don't worry, I love Sabrina and will not hurt her."

"You better not!" Sonya chastised. "Me and Mom and Dad all told you not to settle down, but you didn't listen. So, we'll see how you handle it."

"Speaking of handling things, what's new with you?" Derrick inquired. "The last time we spoke you said you were juggling two men."

Sonya glared at him. "I did not."

He laughed at her reaction. "No, but you

41

did mention this Yusef dude. And then there's Dray still hanging on."

Sonya waved him off. "Yusef yes, Dray maybe. You know Dray and I have a love-hate relationship...but enough about me. You just worry about your own situation."

"Yeah, okay," Derrick said with a chuckle. They'd talked, joked, and laughed as they enjoyed their meals for almost an hour when Sonya looked at the time.

"My, how time flies. I have to get to the station, little brother. Thanks for lunch," she said as she stood up.

Derrick stood to hug her. "You invited me here, so how did I get stuck with the bill?"

"Love you, brother dear," Sonya teased on her way out the restaurant.

Derrick enjoyed the last laugh as the restaurant owner, a crazed Forty-Niners fan, came out and introduced himself and said their meals were on the house.

TRYING TO BE SNEAKY

It had been a week since Sonya and Yusef's great sex. Sonya was on a mission to represent for her vagina and wear something that would have Yusef and his manhood begging for more. She walked into Club Dread like she owned the place, in a turquoise backless dress and matching strappy, stilettos. She made her way over to the bar and spoke to Candy who had been her favorite bartender since she'd began coming to the club.

"Hi, Sonya, your usual?"

"Hey Candy. You already know how I like it."

Sonya smiled as Candy prepared a sour apple martini.

"Damn. You're looking good enough to eat...again."

Sonya turned to face Yusef who was behind her with a sneaky grin on his face.

"Hey you," she replied as she embraced him.

"Damn girl, you're working this outfit. That turquoise is definitely your color, baby. Oh yeah." He winked and said, "Round two later," before heading back to the deejay booth.

Sonya turned back around to take a sip of her drink. Suddenly, her heart thumped against her chest when she spotted Dray on the other side of the bar flirting with the woman seated next to him. Sonya continued to stare at them until Dray scanned the room and locked eyes with hers. Nothing was said between them as Sonya finished her drink and walked off to stand by the deejay booth.

Another night at the club had come to an

end as the music ended and patrons began to leave. Sonya was parked out front waiting for Yusef when Dray emerged from inside the club with the woman he had been talking to earlier. A disgusted look crossed Sonya's face as Dray whispered something in the woman's ear. Dray saw Sonya sitting in her car and headed her way. Sonya nervously checked out the window to be sure Yusef wasn't coming as she lowered the window.

"What are you still doing out here, Sonya?"

"Why? What's it to you?" she asked with an attitude.

"It's obvious, you're not waiting on me or we would have been gone already."

"And clearly, you could care less or *she* would be gone by now," Sonya said as she pointed to the woman that stood by his car.

"Well, I guess we can't always have what we want, so I'll leave you with the deejay.

45

Have a good night, Sonya."

Sonya sat there stunned with no comeback. She had no idea that Dray was aware that she had been seeing Yusef. Feeling defeated, she watched him walk away. Ten minutes later, Yusef finally stepped out carrying his equipment to his truck.

"Are you ready to go?" Sonya yelled out the window in an agitated tone.

"Give me a second. I need to grab a few more things out the club."

Sonya rolled her eyes without him noticing. He was taking longer than last time. She waited fifteen more minutes, only to be told by Yusef, "Sonya, I can't go home with you tonight. Last week, I got caught up in the moment, but the truth is I'm in a relationship right now and we sort of live together."

"How do you *sort of* live with someone?"

"Well, it's my place, but she stays therefrom time to time-with her daughter."

"You have a daughter?"

"No, I don't have any kids. It's her daughter."

There was an uncomfortable silence until Yusef cleared his throat, "I would still like to keep in touch with you, if that's possible?"

Sonya, think before you speak, she told herself. *The man just told you that he's in a relationship, living with someone and her daughter. Drive away and don't look back. Don't give in!*

A few seconds passed before she blurted out, "You can call me."

* * *

Donna didn't know what to think? It was the first time Yusef hadn't initiated making love to her. She'd walked into the living room wearing a sexy lace negligee while he was playing music on his turntables. She wrapped her arms around his waist and began to place light kisses on his back. He was trying to mix and tilted his head to the side to count the right beat on when to bring in the next song. Donna could feel him pulling away. She couldn't figure out why he was acting like that. Could it be that he didn't want to be bothered?

"Donna, let me do this. I'm trying out some new stuff to play in the club on Saturday."

"I know. But, I thought with Katina out we could enjoy this time to ourselves."

Once Yusef switched to another song, he lifted her head to his and began to kiss her, trying to please her. It was different for him though. His eyes were closed and he could only think of Sonya and how soft her body felt next to his. It wasn't feeling right with Donna as he broke away from her embrace.

"What's going on Yusef? In the past couple of weeks, you've been distant. Tell me, what's bothering you?"

Yusef stopped the music. They needed to talk. He loved Donna, but there was something missing in their relationship and it was only fair to tell her how he was feeling.

"I need some space."

"What's that supposed to mean?" Donna asked, instantly taking offense. "We've been together for six years and not once have I pressured you into doing anything you didn't want to do. Now all of a sudden, you need space. Tell me Yusef, what is it?" Donna swallowed hard, "Are you seeing someone else?"

Yusef wasn't about to admit that he was beginning to enjoy the pleasure of another woman. He chose his words carefully, "I just...I don't know. I want to make sure it's right before we both regret something later in our lives. That might not make sense to you, but I want to figure out where I want to be in life. You already have your daughter and I always wanted a child of my own one day."

Tears swelled in Donna's eyes. The words she'd dreaded were finally said out loud. After giving birth to her daughter, the doctor had informed her of a tumor on her uterus that needed to be removed, which meant no more kids for her. She felt bad. She loved Yusef dearly, but a child was the one thing that she would never be able to give him.

"If space is what you need, I'll go pack my bags, because space is what you'll get." With nothing left to say, Donna walked out the room.

MIXED EMOTIONS

As the season progressed, Derrick's game adjusted and he was doing extremely well. Along with that, he was gaining notoriety, which came with lots of attention, popularity, and fame. Sabrina admired Derrick as she stood outside the locker room and watched as her man soaked up the limelight after another game win. However, she frowned when Megan Richards approached him. Derrick smiled at whatever was being said. Sabrina couldn't deny that bothered her. Granted, Megan was a sports reporter, but she hung around Derrick more than normal and Sabrina had started to take notice.

"Hey baby," Derrick said as he walked

over to Sabrina. "I'm going to be a little late tonight."

"Oh." Sabrina raised a brow. "Why? What's going on?"

Derrick's eyes shifted a bit. "It's just something I need to handle, but I won't be long," he said with a kiss.

Sabrina was skeptical, but kept her cool. Sabrina knew she had to trust Derrick, so instead of second-guessing and questioning him on his whereabouts, she left it alone, at least for the moment.

"Alright Derrick, I'll see you when you get home."

Sabrina pulled out her cell phone and called Renee to see if she was home. She was in her feelings and needed her best friend.

* * *

"Hey girl, what are you doing here?" Renee moved to the side to let Sabrina enter. "Where's your man?"

"He had something to do."

"So why the long face? You can't breathe without him?" Renee joked.

Sabrina ignored the snide remark. "How are you? Where's Bradsen?"

Renee shrugged her shoulders. "I don't know. He had to step out, as well."

"Wow, I love what you've done to the place." Sabrina admired the trendy new updated kitchen that was redesigned with stainless steel appliances. The living room had been repainted and decorated with stylish furniture.

"Thanks." Renee smiled. "Courtesy of Bradsen Myers. He had his interior designer redecorate every room. Your old bedroom was turned into a cozy home office.

"So, how are things, Bri? I know you. What's on your mind? What's going on with you and Derrick?"

"I don't know," she whined. "Lately, he's

been acting weird around the house. He's officially a superstar now and I'm okay with that part. But, it's the whispering into the phone, the walking out to take his calls in another room. Or, my new favorite one, 'Something came up; I'll be back soon.' Those are the things that I have a problem with."

"What are you saying? You don't trust him?"

"I do trust him. It's the other women that I don't trust, especially that reporter Megan Richards from Channel Five Sports Edition. Every time I turn around she's there, smiling, and giggling in his face," Sabrina said in a huff. "She's not fooling anyone, she wants Derrick. I can tell-"

Renee cut her short. "Okay, stop with the insecurity. It's not cute on you."

"Whatever," Sabrina said as she rolled her eyes.

"Don't even try it. Derrick is a good man,

despite the reputation of his profession. I think he really loves you and only you. Trust me, he wouldn't have asked you to move in with him if he wanted to cheat on you."

Sabrina cracked a smile. "I guess you're right, but girl it's hard with these females. They are professional groupies."

"Yes they are, but remember you already have what they want. Don't make it easy for them to get it."

"Thanks, Renee. I knew coming here would make me feel better. But enough about me, let's talk about you."

Renee pointed to herself. "What about me?"

"What's going on with you and Bradsen? I know you wanted to take things slow, but this is a little too slow-even for my taste. You do realize you have a good man too, right? How long do you think you are going to be able to continue stringing him along before he gets tired of it?"

Renee hissed, "I'm not stringing him along. Besides Bradsen knows I need more time."

"Time for what? So you can self-sabotage the relationship and push him away again?" Renee sat quietly. "I never asked you this because I had assumed you were fine with the way things ended with Kayron. But are you truly over him?"

Renee stared at Sabrina for the longest time before she burst out laughing. "Girl, yes I'm done with him." Then her face turned serious. "I'm just scared," she quietly admitted.

"Finally, you're ready to talk to me." Sabrina threw up her hands. "Tell me bestie, why are you scared?"

Tears swelled Renee eyes. "Bradsen loves me so much and I do love him, too, but his family-they feel the opposite and I don't know how we can make it work?"

"Since when do you care about what others think about you?"

Normally Renee wouldn't care, but she was concerned about Bradsen and his relationship with his family.

"You saw his reaction the other day," Renee said, referring to Bradsen's attitude when they were headed back from the party. "He's really having a rough time dealing with this. I keep trying to tell him you can't make something be there that's not. He can't understand how they can overlook Kayron being around, but still have issues with me. I know the difference is because Kayron is married to Brenda."

"How is that different? Two wrongs don't make a right?"

"I get that. However, she's still his wife and also Cynthia's sister."

"I'm sorry, I must be missing the point

because aren't Bradsen and Jacksen brothers?" Sabrina asked confused.

"Yes, but-"

Sabrina paused, giving her an exasperated look. "Stop making excuses on why you shouldn't be with Bradsen. You are making this more difficult than it has to be. Why can't you accept the fact that he wants you, for you? Nothing more, nothing less. He deserves better than how you're treating him, Renee."

Sabrina was always team Bradsen from the first day she met him, so the whole back and forth between Renee and him was getting old.

Renee knew Sabrina was right. She took a deep breath before saying, "You're right, Bri. Maybe Bradsen and I should get away for a few days and go somewhere to work things out."

"Yeah, that sounds like a great idea. You

two should make that happen-and soon."

Renee shrugged her shoulders. "We'll see."

* * *

"Thanks for meeting me here, B." Derrick greeted Bradsen as he walked up to the family-owned jewelry store located inside the Crocker Galleria. The Galleria was a beautiful tri-level area in Union Square surrounded by glass framed windows that had an array of high-end specialty shops.

"No problem," Bradsen said as they exchanged fist bumps. He reached for the door handle. "Are you ready to go in?"

Derrick paused to steady his breathing. "Yes, I'm ready...I'm ready to do this," he nervously repeated.

"It's okay," Bradsen assured him. "I felt the same way when I picked out the ring I used to propose to Renee."

"Yeah, but didn't she turn you down?"

Derrick teased.

"She did. However, I haven't given up on her accepting my marriage proposal one of these days," Bradsen said, hopeful.

Derrick shook his head. "Man, I don't know how you deal with it. I would be suffering if I knew the woman I loved kept me at arm's length."

Bradsen's smile wavered a bit. "Renee has every right to feel the way she does."

"Does she?" Derrick quizzed. "Don't get me wrong, B, I'm just an outsider looking in. I only recently met Renee and didn't know about the drama you two had going on. But what I do know is...life is too short to be playing games. You're either going to be together, or you're not."

Derrick quickly reverted back to the original topic. "Anyway, like I said, I'm ready to do this. I may be young, but Sabrina Brown is the woman of my dreams. Right after my away game, I'm going to ask her to marry me."

Derrick then reached for the store's door handle and entered. Bradsen didn't say a word as he trailed behind him. He understood how Derrick felt, since he-himself-had only dated Renee for a short time before he proposed to her. In his heart, Bradsen knew that Renee would eventually come around. He didn't know when, but he wasn't ready to move on, at least not without her. There had to be a way to reach her and he had to come up with a plan. Maybe they could go on a trip somewhere. Bradsen smiled inwardly as he knew of a nice secluded spot.

FRIENDS, LOVERS, AND

ENEMIES

Derrick had his first away game in Miami against the Dolphins. After losing their first game, he was back at the hotel seated at the bar alone. He sat quietly deep in thought when a familiar voice said from behind him, "Tough game today. Can I buy you a drink?"

Derrick turned and there stood Megan Richards in a black, low cut mini-dress that looked absolutely stunning on her along with a pair of high heel strappy sandals. He couldn't take his eyes off of her as he swallowed hard.

"Megan, what are you doing here?" Before

Megan could respond, Derrick continued. "Let me guess you were in the neighborhood."

Megan smiled and took a seat next to him, "I'll have what he's having," she said to the bartender that had approached them.

Megan returned her attention back to Derrick and scooted her chair closer to his. "Actually, I'm here for you. I thought you could use a friend."

"Thanks, I appreciate that-a friend that just so happened to be in the area."

"Derrick, why won't you talk to me?"

"I do talk to you. Every time you put your recorder in my face."

"You know what I mean. Why haven't you tried to get to know me?"

"What's that supposed to mean?" The edge of her arrogance surprised him.

Megan leaned in closer. "I'm attracted to you and I think you know that," she said as she touched his leg.

"Megan, I'm flattered, but I'm not interested. I'm in a committed relationship with a woman that I'm in love with."

"I respect that, but you can't fault a girl for trying," she replied as she kissed him lightly on the cheek.

By the end of the night, Derrick and Megan parted as friends, but not before an unknown person that stood in the distance snapped a few pictures of the two of them together. Little did Derrick know these photos would be posted on the internet and would later come back to haunt him.

* * *

It had been a long day for Sabrina. Ever since it leaked that she was dating Derrick, her online perfume and cologne business was in high demand. She was about to log off her laptop when she decided to check her email. She strolled through advertisements and celebrity gossip to get to her inbox. While doing so she immediately saw a photo that caught her attention. In the photo, Megan Richards had her arm around Derrick St. Jermaine as she kissed him on the cheek.

"What the-?" Sabrina cursed to herself. The attached article was titled "Star Rookie Linebacker up Close and Personal with Sports Reporter". "That lying dog, I can't believe he would do this to me?" Sabrina said as she began to cry. She slammed the laptop shut and noticed the time. Derrick would be landing soon. She grabbed her purse and keys and headed out the door.

Thirty minutes later, Sabrina was parked outside the airport terminal, waiting to pick up Derrick. She tried her best to steady her breathing as he walked out.

"Hey beautiful," Derrick said as he hugged her. "It's great to be home. I've missed you." He felt her body tense and asked, "Are you okay?"

Sabrina wasn't one to cause a public scene, so she smiled through clenched teeth and got back in the car. Derrick had no idea what was wrong as he tried to make small talk, but it was no use as Sabrina remained quiet. Finally after the long drive in silence, they arrived home. Derrick closed the door behind him and reached for Sabrina.

She took a step back. "Don't touch me."

"What is the matter with you? Why are you acting like this?" Derrick asked, clueless.

That infuriated her more. "Derrick, I told you not to test me, and what do you do? You go sneaking around behind my back with Megan Richards. I saw the photos of you two in Miami together," Sabrina spat before she started to cry again.

"Baby, it's not what you think," Derrick's voice softened. "Whatever you saw, nothing happened."

"It didn't look like nothing to me," she retorted. "Megan has wanted you all along and this is exactly why-"

"Yeah I know." Derrick cut her short and admitted that Megan was upfront about her true intentions that past weekend when she approached him at the bar. "I made it very clear that I wasn't interested in her. End of story."

"Okay, if that were the case, where was this kiss on the cheek coming from? You expect me to believe that's all that happened?"

"Yes. Why would I risk our relationship like that? Look, Sabrina, I know it's hard for you to trust me right now, but think about it. Why would I do this to you? To us? Baby, I love you so much, you have to believe that I wouldn't do anything to jeopardize our relationship."

Sabrina didn't say a word and stormed off

in a huff. Derrick stood there dumbfounded. He wanted to run after her, but instead he immediately pulled out his cell phone to search for answers. He was furious when he came across the pictures and saw for himself. He quickly went out on the patio and called Megan.

* * *

Megan returned home from Miami. It had been a waste of a trip when Derrick had turned down her romantic advances. She hadn't expected that to happen. Usually, when most new players were away, they wouldn't think twice about it. That's how she was able to snag Ben Williams when he was a rookie. The only difference was he had a wife and when their thing ended on a bad note, he felt betrayed by Megan for leaving him. However, Derrick was different than Ben. He didn't judge her for coming on to him and he didn't push her away. He simply made it known that he wasn't interested. Megan sat her luggage down in her two-bedroom loft apartment when her cell phone rang. She recognized the number and smiled. *Maybe he wasn't so different from the rest after all,* she thought.

"Hello Derrick," Megan said sweetly into the phone.

"Megan, what have you done? Why are there pictures of us on the internet?"

"Derrick, I just landed an hour ago. What are you talking about?"

Derrick filled her in on all the details.

"What?"

Megan was shocked. She had no idea that happened. She wasn't even on the schedule to work. She went out to see Derrick on her own time, so there was no traveling crew with her. Megan got an eerie feeling to think someone was out there possibly tracking her every move.

"I'm sorry Derrick, but I didn't do this. My trip to Miami was strictly personal."

"Okay, well if you didn't do it, then we need to get to the bottom of who did?"

Derrick hung up the phone still enraged. It was late, so he went back into the house to get some rest. He would tackle the mystery the next day.

* * *

Sonya and Yusef had enjoyed a night out at Sundance Cinemas in the lower Pacific Heights District. The multiplex dine-in movie theatre offered reserved seating in plush reclining chairs. It was a twenty-one and older establishment that served alcohol and had plenty of snacks to choose from. Once the movie was over, they decided to take a ride on the cable car to Fisherman's Wharf to stroll around Pier 39.

It was a clear night, considering the weather was a bit cool around the fall season.

They walked along the boardwalk taking in all the sights and even played a few arcade games before calling it a night. Sonya had truly enjoyed herself. It was a welcome distraction from their usual wee hours in the morning sexual activities. Once, she returned home, she had invited Yusef to stay but he declined. He wanted her to know that it was more than just sex with him. She kissed him goodnight and headed inside. It was a great ending to a perfect date. As soon as Sonya pulled off her shoes and coat, her cell phone rang.

"Sonya," her assistant, Maureen, said into the phone. "Sorry to bother you on your day off. I called to inform you of some breaking news that just came into the newsroom."

Sonya could tell it was serious by the tone of Maureen's voice. Maureen wasn't her usual bubbly self. Sonya began asking questions. "What happened? Where was it?

When did it take place? Are there any casualties? Do they need me at the scene?"

Her assistant paused to take a deep breath. She knew this particular story would hit Sonya hard. "You're not needed on the scene, but I'm sorry to tell you it's about Dray McKinnis."

Sonya's heart began to race. "What about him?"

"He was involved in a warehouse fire when the roof collapsed." Sonya gasped in shock as her assistant continued. "He's in intensive care at Kaiser Medical Center. I'll text you the rest of the details if you want to get to him."

Sonya ended the call, dazed. She hadn't heard from Dray since the night they'd argued outside of the club. She had no idea what was going on with him, but to hear that type of news was really freaking her out. Her mind raced with all kinds of crazy thoughts.

For a brief moment, she was unable to speak. She leaned her body against the wall and fought back tears. After she regained her composure, she was too distraught to call the hospital so she immediately dialed Brenda.

"Hello."

"What took you so long to answer the phone and why are you so out of breath?"

Brenda smiled at the thought of making love to her husband as she rolled over and glanced lovingly at Kayron who was fast asleep.

"Never mind that," Sonya said when Brenda didn't respond. "I'm just glad you're home because something bad has happened to Dray."

"Wait. Hold on." Brenda got up from the bed. "Now, what happened to Dray?"

"I don't have all the details. My assistant called and told me there had been a warehouse fire and the roof collapsed and that Dray was in the hospital."

"Hospital!" Brenda shouted in her ear. "Oh my God, is he-"

Sonya didn't let her finish the sentence. "I have no idea, but I didn't want to go alone just in case it's something more than I can handle. Do you mind coming with me?"

"Sonya, you know I got your back. Do we know which hospital he's in?"

"Yes, he's at Kaiser."

"Okay, let me tell Kayron and I will be there to pick you up shortly."

"Thanks, soror."

"Hang in there. I'm on my way."

* * *

Dray sat up in the hospital bed with an IV in his arm, thankful to be alive to see another day. The fire station had received a call that there was a fire that was burning out of control at an abandoned industrial warehouse in Alameda County. After they

74

checked for civilians and determined the building was unsafe, he and his partner got out of there just in the nick of time before the roof caved in. They both suffered from smoke inhalation and a few minor scratches, but nothing serious. He knew the dangers of being a firefighter, but he enjoyed the thrill and excitement.

Dray wanted to call Sonya to tell her that he was okay. He was sure she had heard the news. On occasion, the media made it sound worse than it appeared. He had hoped she would come and be by his side, but that was wishful thinking on his part. It was obvious she was where she wanted to be-in the arms of someone else. But, after all they'd shared, the history they had, and the secret love untold, he didn't want to lose her. He'd always wanted to tell her how much he loved her, but always felt like it was never the right time.

Dray picked up his phone to call Sonya, but he quickly put it down. His mind kept telling him he should make the call, but the fear of rejection would not allow him to. Mentally defeated, he reached for the pitcher of water that was located on the end table at the foot of his bed. He still hadn't got all of his strength back, so he strained. While in mid reach for the pitcher, Sonya and Brenda walked through the door.

"Here, let me get that for you." Sonya hurried and grabbed the pitcher and poured Dray a cup of water.

"Thanks," he said surprised. "I wasn't expecting to see you."

"How are you feeling?" Brenda asked from behind Sonya.

"A little banged up, but you know me, I'm strong." He smiled.

"Well, we're just glad you're okay," said Sonya. "According to the nurse it could have been a lot worse if you hadn't run out the building when you did."

Brenda glanced over her shoulder at Sonya. "I'm going to walk out and give you two a minute. Take your time Sonya. You can meet me in the waiting room when you're ready."

Brenda smiled at Dray. "I'm glad you're alright. Do you need anything?"

"Nope, I'm good. You brought me what I needed," he said as he directed his attention back to Sonya.

Sonya pulled up a chair and sat down next to Dray's bed when Brenda walked out.

"I'm really glad you're here, Sonya."

"Dray, please," Sonya said with an exaggerated sigh. "We may not be together, but I love you and can't imagine losing you."

"Thank you, baby. You're the only real woman that I can count on. You understand me and never turned your back on me."

Sonya reached for Dray's hand. Now was his chance to tell her how he really felt about her. How much he loved her...How much he wanted to be with her.

Meanwhile, Sonya and her thoughts debated on whether to share with him that she and Yusef were becoming serious. She decided it wasn't the time. He was already in enough pain. Instead, they sat in silence for a while, both afraid of what to tell the other. Friends, lovers, and enemies, saying goodbye to each other didn't fall into either one of those categories.

UNEXPECTED REACTION

The next morning Derrick woke up still wondering where the photos had come from. With Sabrina still not talking to him, he was determined to find out. Not knowing where to turn, he called his sister to see if she could help him.

"Hello," Sonya whispered into the phone. She had spent the night at Brenda and Kayron's house after visiting Dray in the hospital.

"Hey sis, why aren't you at work?"

"It was a long night. Dray's in the hospital and Brenda went with me, so I stayed over her house."

"The hospital, is he okay?"

"Yeah, he was involved in a bad warehouse fire. He has a few bumps and bruises, but he'll live." She'd detected the urgency in his voice. "So, what's up with you?"

"Well," he sighed. "I need your help with something."

"Oh boy, Derrick, what have you done?"

"I can show you better than I can tell you."

"It's that bad?"

"Let's just say Sabrina's not talking to me."

"Man. Okay I'll get dressed. Since I didn't drive, do you want to come and pick me up?"

"Okay. If I remember correctly, Brenda stays near Lakeside Park?"

"Yes, I'll text you the address. See you soon."

* * *

Sonya needed a pick-me-up, so Derrick stopped at the nearest Starbucks. While she waited for her Caramel Macchiato, Derrick showed her the pictures. Sonya handed him back his phone and without saying a word, she punched him in the arm.

"Ouch," he rubbed the spot she'd just hit. "What was that for?"

"That's for me saying I told you so."

"But nothing happened!"

"I believe you," she said matter-of-factly.

"You do?" he asked with a raised eyebrow.

"Megan is messy. That's why I kept saying watch out for her. It wouldn't surprise me if she was the one who posted those photos herself."

"I already spoke to her about it and she claims it wasn't her. So, will you help me find out, because I can't propose to Sabrina until this gets resolved?"

Sonya choked on her drink, spilling a little on her sleeve. "Propose? As in marriage?"

"Yes. I love her, sis, and I won't let anyone ruin this for me."

"You're serious about this?"

"You're damn right, I'm serious." Derrick pulled out the canary-yellow, princess cut diamond engagement ring with smaller diamonds around the edges. He still had the ring in his pocket from the previous night.

"Nice! Well, lucky for you brother dear, I love this kind of investigative work. I'll get started on finding out more information. I'll keep you posted," Sonya said and laughed at her own joke, but Derrick didn't find it funny as he pulled out of the parking lot.

* * *

After Derrick dropped Sonya home, she took a shower, got dressed in a burgundy neck-tie dress with over the knee boots, and headed back out to her job where she had more resources available to her. She walked into the Channel Five building, checked in with security, and then rode the elevator up to the fifth floor. She stepped into the newsroom and went to her cubicle to turn on her computer.

"Hi Sonya." Her assistant, Maureen, greeted her from across the desk. "How's Mr. McKinnis?"

"Dray is fine and he's home recovering now. He should be back to work in no time."

"That's good news," Maureen said as she swung around in her chair.

"Are you ready to get to work?" Sonya turned back around to face her computer.

"Yes ma'am, what you got?"

"I have the latest developing story."

Maureen looked at her perplexed. "Sonya, you don't research news anymore, you mainly report it."

"Yes, I know that's what I have you for. But, the funny thing about this story, it's a personal matter and the source came from this station."

Sonya filled Maureen in on what was happening.

"Why would the editor approve something like that when he knows the two of you are related? That doesn't make any sense. Are you sure it's from here?" Maureen said, doubtful.

"I bet it was Megan Richards."

"I understand your frustration, especially if it came from here. But how? Megan wasn't on assignment last weekend and hadn't logged into the database to upload anything. She couldn't have done it."

Sonya cut her eyes at Maureen.

"I'm in no way defending her I'm just stating the facts. I realize there's bad blood between you two, but this reminds me of that other player this happened to, where Megan was involved. What was his name? Ben somebody..." Maureen tried to think.

"Oh that's right," Sonya recalled, "Williams, Ben Williams." Sonya turned back around to study the pictures once again.

"What am I missing?" she said to herself. Suddenly it came to her when she noticed something different than she had before.

"Maureen, take a look at this." Maureen took a closer glance at the screen.

After their discovery, they both looked up at each other, baffled, until Maureen spoke first, "That's really strange. I'll get our sister station on the line for you."

"No need, I'll make the call myself."

85

She stepped away and found an empty conference room where Sonya called her confidential contact at Channel Five's sister station in Oakland. It was times like these she was glad to work with someone that she could discreetly trust for answers.

"Hello, it's me. I need a favor."

"What's up?"

"A story was released from your station to us about Megan Richards and Derrick St. Jermaine. I'm trying to track down the source. Can you get that for me?"

"Sure, hold on...Okay here it is...It was an Officer Julia Williams."

"Officer Julia Williams?" Sonya repeated silently, "Okay thanks. I owe you one."

Sonya hung up the phone wondering why that name sounded so familiar. Finally, it hit her. She quickly dialed Megan.

"Megan, where are you?" Sonya said,

rushed, "We need to talk."

"I know why you're calling, and 'No' it wasn't me who posted those photos of me and your brother," she said sarcastically.

"Yeah, I know it wasn't you and I just found out who the source was. We need to talk face-to-face."

That instantly got Megan's attention. "Yeah sure, I was just leaving the gym. Are you at the job?"

"Yes, I'm in the conference room. I'll see you soon."

* * *

Megan changed out her gym clothes and into a black belted pant-suit with pointed toe heels and she made her way back to work. She couldn't believe Sonya had found information so fast. Although, she and Sonya weren't the best of friends, Megan had to give her props for being good at finding stories. Megan was still trying to piece it all together as she went to the conference room.

"Megan, you already know this isn't a social visit," Sonya said as she closed the door when Megan took a seat. "You're here because I'm helping my brother clear up this incident between you two. So please don't waste my time and just give it to me straight. Who is Officer Julia Williams and what is her connection to you?"

Megan gasped when she heard that name. She sat there frozen as her mind drifted off into space.

"Megan? Megan?" Sonya repeated, trying to get her attention. "Who is she?"

Sonya was taken aback a bit when Megan started to cry. She hadn't expected that reaction. Megan was considered one of the guys, a beast when it came to dealing with the guys from various NFL teams. In a male-dominated sport, it was harder for women to break through; it was even harder to be taken serious. They had to be strong because there was no room for emotion. Seeing Megan's tears made Sonya soften her voice, "I'm sorry to upset you. It's just that, this is important to Derrick and me to find out."

Megan hung her head low. She had buried this story in the back of her mind or so she thought. Never once did she think it would resurface as she began to speak.

"Two years ago, I had an affair with an NFL player named Ben Williams. He was Officer Julia Williams' late husband."

"Oh wow," Sonya said, stunned, "It was reported that he got shot and killed last year?"

"He did," Megan confirmed. "What the media failed to mention was that it was one of his mistresses that killed him. Ben had numerous affairs. The reason we broke up was because I found out I wasn't the only one. Somehow, Julia found out about us. She blames me for his infidelity and has had it out for me ever since."

"But, why go after Derrick, too? He has more to lose than you?"

"That part I can't answer, because she wouldn't know Derrick unless she met him recently or something." Megan regained her composure and stood to leave.

"Thanks Megan for your time," Sonya said as she shook her head. The mystery had been solved. Derrick St. Jermaine and Officer Williams met at the dinner party. It was time for Sonya to go fill Derrick and Sabrina in on what she knew.

* * *

Derrick and Sabrina sat in the living room waiting for Sonya to arrive. She had said she needed to see both of them together. She knew Sabrina was still mad at Derrick and she didn't want him to know beforehand.

She felt that would defeat the purpose.

"How's my favorite couple doing?" Sonya said as she entered the living room and hugged both of them. She could see the stress lines on Derrick's face. Sabrina on the other hand showed no signs of distress, but she could sense the tension between them.

Sonya got right to the point. "Okay, you guys, here's what I know. The pictures were posted by an Officer Julia Williams."

"Who is that?" Derrick wanted to know. The name sounded familiar, but he didn't remember from where.

However, Sabrina had a different look on her face at the mention of the name. She knew that name all too well. In fact, she would never forget it. Sabrina finally spoke up, "I know exactly who she is. But my question is why? We haven't done anything to her, but she always seems to be in our business?" Sabrina was visibly upset.

"Okay, I'm lost," Derrick said as he shook his head.

Sonya looked over at Sabrina, "I don't quite understand what you mean either, but I do know that she was trying to get back at Megan Richards."

"Megan," Sabrina blurted out. "What does she have to do with this? This is about Renee and Kayron."

"No sister dear, this is about Officer Williams seeking revenge on Megan because she's still bitter at her for having an affair with her late husband, Ben Williams."

"Really? That would explain a lot." Sabrina said sitting there deep in thought.

Derrick butted in. "I'm still trying to figure out where I know this officer from. I haven't had a run-in with the law."

Sabrina filled him in. "Derrick, she was at the dinner party that we went to with Bradsen and Renee. Remember, she came in with Kayron and Brenda."

"Oh okay. But why did you say she was in our business?"

Sabrina took a deep breath before saying. "Back when Renee was having an affair with Kayron and he vanished without a trace, I was trying to help her find him. I called the Oakland precinct for Renee and Officer Williams answered and was the one that told me he had passed away. Then in a bitter, almost angry voice, she told me he was buried at Sunset Memorial Cemetery. I don't know for sure," Sabrina added, "But after hearing this, I can pretty much bet that's where her husband is laid to rest."

"Wow, talk about a small world," Derrick said.

Sabrina finally cracked a smile as that was usually her line. She couldn't count the number of times she had said those words this past year dealing with Renee and her drama.

"Well guys, it sounds like this Officer Williams has deep-rooted issues and we won't try to figure them out now, but hopefully she can eventually move on and be happy one day in her own life," said Sonya. "I was able to get the pictures removed and if that's all, I'm going to hit the road."

Derrick hugged Sonya tight. "Thanks, sis, for your help. I love you."

"Thanks, Sonya," Sabina said as she hugged her next. Sonya whispered to her during their embrace. "Don't give up on my brother. He needs you."

Derrick closed the door behind Sonya once she walked out.

He reached for Sabrina, "Baby, come here." He was happy that Sabrina didn't pull away. "I love you so much."

"I love you, too, Derrick. And I apologize for not really trusting you. I let my insecurity over another woman get the better of me."

"Bri, I told you baby, you are going to have to trust me in order for our relationship to work. This won't be the last time we will be tested by outside sources."

"I know," Sabrina said low.

Derrick lifted her chin and kissed her lips. As much as he loved Sabrina, he knew it wasn't the time for him to propose marriage to her. He wanted them to work on building a solid foundation first. Once that was strong, then he would happily get down on bended knee and make her his wife. Until then, Derrick took her by the hand and led her upstairs to their bedroom to make up for lost time.

EMOTIONAL ROLLERCOASTER

Over the next seven months, Sonya spent her time doing exactly what Brenda had told her not to do and that was wear her heart on her sleeve. Yusef had been wonderful. They'd been spending every possible moment together. Whether it was at the club, each other's house or just hanging out, they were together. Sonya was enjoying every minute of it. While she was falling in love with him, he told her that he still had feelings for his ex-girlfriend and thought she should know. Why wasn't she surprised?

The more involved they got, the more complicated their relationship was. Yusef had just gotten out of a long-term relationship, which was understandable to Sonya. But what wasn't was that he acted like Sonya was the reason for his world tearing apart. She couldn't force him to want her and if he wasn't ready, what could she do? Yusef wasn't trying to get caught up in a new relationship right then and she couldn't blame him. She didn't want that any more than he did. She was at the height of her career.

Then there was Dray. Sonya's heart kept telling her she hadn't resolved her feelings for him. But now that she was all wrapped up in Yusef, he wanted to slow things down a bit and was beginning to push her away. What was the point in fighting if she was waging a losing battle? She could take back her time and effort, but she couldn't take back the love she had for him. Brenda tried to reassure her to have patience and hang in there, but where was *there* when she didn't even know what she'd been hanging on to?

"It's so good to see you." Brenda hugged Sonya before they entered the Mexican restaurant. Sonya made sure Brenda was okay with the wait. Be it lunch or dinner, no matter what time of the day it was, LaTaqueria on Mission Street was always crowded, but their various burritos and tacos were worth the wait.

"So, what's up, girl?" Brenda asked while they stood in line. "It seems like forever since we last talked. How's work? Since, that's the only time I seem to get to see you now is when you're reporting the news."

"It's going great! I don't have any complaints. It's funny how my job is keeping me happier than my personal life."

"I take it things with you and Yusef are a little crazy?"

"A little crazy. You think?" Sonya sighed. "I'm just about fed up with him being torn between me and his ex-girlfriend. How did I let myself get so caught up in him? It's like my world revolves around him now."

"Nine and a half inches happened, remember?" Brenda broke out laughing.

By the time they made it to the front of the line, Sonya ordered two carnitas tacos filled with meat, black beans, guacamole and sour cream. Brenda settled on the super burrito that was jam-packed with carne asada, pinto beans, avocado, and cheese. They found an empty picnic table near the back and resumed their conversation.

"What's the latest with Kayron? The last time we spoke you two had rekindled your love life. I knew you were glowing for a reason. I'm glad somebody's happy," she whined.

"Kayron and I are great. Sonya, if

you're not happy, then why are you still dating Yusef? Is it really that serious?"

"I don't know. Maybe I feel this way because I'm not seeing anyone else."

"You haven't heard from Dray?"

"Once after he got out the hospital, I called to see how he was doing. It was brief, he was fine and that was basically it. I really didn't have anything to say and he was pretty quiet, so we hung up and haven't spoken since."

"That's been a while now. But in his defense, he does know you're dating Yusef so he could be giving you space. Do you miss him?"

Sonya would be lying if she didn't say she had, but those days she didn't want to think about Dray. She was really trying to make it work between her and Yusef.

"Well, Sonya. I never say I told you so, but how many times did I tell you to be careful with Yusef?"

"Yeah, yeah, I know." Sonya waved her hand in the air.

"That's your fault, you let his good sex go to your head," she joked.

They both laughed and then settled down to finish their meal. Sonya missed hanging out with Brenda, but how easy it was for them to forget each other when they both had men in their lives.

ONE LINE OR TWO

Sonya stopped by the drugstore to pick up a pregnancy test before heading home after work. She got the idea that she might be pregnant over the weekend when they were at the club having a great time. Towards the end of the night, she started to vomit. Sonya had been going to Club Dread for as long as she could remember and the bartender, Candy, always served her the same drink-a sour apple martini. But Saturday night she felt nauseous. Talk about embarrassing, she was grateful that Yusef was there to drive her home. Now she found herself awaiting the results of a two-minute test. Neither of them had discussed having children nor had she thought about getting pregnant by Yusef. He had been her only sex partner, so there would be no doubt that he was the father. That was the longest two minutes of her life. She glanced at the clock, it was finally time to check to see if there was one line or two.

When Sonya saw two lines, she knew that in less than nine months she would become someone's mother and Yusef would be a father. Her first thought was what was she going to do? Her first initial thought was even if she was going to have the baby. Her relationship with Yusef wasn't where she wanted it, even though she was physically healthy and financially stable. With or without Yusef, she had faith that she and her baby would be fine. She couldn't believe she had second-guessed herself. Maybe she did have choices, but there was only one choice for her and that was she was going to take care of her responsibility. Life was too short not to experience the miracle of life. Plus,

Sonya was so in love with Yusef. No matter what happened with their relationship, she would be happy to have this bond with him for life. She would be giving him something no other woman had given him-his firstborn.

How do you tell a guy that you've only known for a year that you're pregnant? Sonya didn't know but she only had a few minutes to figure it out before Yusef arrived. She was scared.

During the time they'd been together she had been more committed than he was. He was still torn between two women. He had a lot of history with Donna and a short story with Sonya. He'd practically helped raise Donna's daughter for the six years they were together, and now he was about to be told that he would be having a child of his own. Sonya tried to mentally prepare herself for the stress as she held back the tears.

"Hey, baby." Yusef saw her sitting on the

sofa in the living room. "What's up?"

He would be in a good mood, she thought to herself.

He walked over to kiss her. "You ready to go?"

"Go where?"

"You forgot? We were going to dinner. That's why I'm here so early."

"Oh, can we go some other time? Something has come up that we need to discuss."

"Is everything okay?"

Yusef hadn't been in the door five minutes and she was already beginning to cry.

"I have something to show you."

"What is it?"

She walked upstairs with him right behind her. When they got to her bedroom, she immediately pointed to the vanity. He walked over and saw the home pregnancy test sitting there. He picked it up slowly and looked over at her. By her reaction it could only mean one thing.

"So, you're pregnant, huh?"

Sonya nodded her head. She couldn't anticipate his words. She couldn't read his expression as Yusef stood there, stunned. He didn't know what to say. Deep down inside he knew he wanted a family but wasn't sure he wanted one at this time.

"Are you going to have it?"

Again, she nodded her head. He reached out and grabbed her hand and pulled her close into his chest.

"Don't cry, Sonya, we'll get through this."

That's comforting to know. At least he didn't walk out, she thought as she let her tears flow.

* * *

A few hours later, Yusef returned home to gather his thoughts. While deep in thought, he felt the need to call Donna.

"She's what?" Donna yelled through the phone. "I thought I was giving you space to clear your mind. Not involve yourself in another relationship. Now you're telling me that she's pregnant? I don't believe this. How could you do this to us? Do you love her?"

Yusef didn't know how to answer that question. He thought back to the day that he wanted to get to know Sonya St. Jermaine. Loving her had never entered his mind.

"I care about her and my unborn child. I don't know what's going to happen? We haven't really sat down and talked about it yet, I just know she's having the baby and I wanted you to know."

Donna held the phone as the tears flowed. She had nothing more to say. She didn't want answers of why he did it? What happened between them? She just wanted him to be a man and take care of his responsibility. He got what he finally wanted. There was no need for them to go on.

Donna swallowed hard, "You've got what you wanted, Yusef. Now, do the right thing. Figure out what's best for the two of you and don't call me until you do." Donna released the line. She didn't yell and she didn't tell Yusef to have a nice life. No, she just took another step back to give him time to see what he was giving up.

SURPRISE, SURPRISE

Sonya decided not to have the baby's sex revealed during her ultrasound. The most important thing was that the baby was fine and she didn't have a preference of what she was having. What was the point in having a preference anyway? It wasn't like she could change the gender of the child, but Yusef didn't seem to agree. He wanted to know so he could start buying stuff for the baby. They were sitting at the dining room table having dinner at Yusef's house when she looked over at him and smiled.

"What are you thinking about?" he asked, taking the last bite of his lasagna.

"I think we should move in together. I have plenty of space and it would be nice to have you around to help care for the baby."

Yusef was speechless. He stared at her as if she had spoken a foreign language.

"Hello, earth to Yusef. What do you think?"

"Sonya, I know you mean well, but we've been moving way too fast. You're looking for stability and I'm just not ready for that, but I'll be there for the baby."

"That's just it! You'll be there for the baby, but what about me? I'm getting so tired of you still having doubts about us and where you want to be."

"Sonya, I love you. Look at where I am now?"

"I understand that, but where are you when you're not with me? Where does your heart lie then? This is all new for me and it should be a happy time for us. Instead, I'm stressing trying to figure things out."

"Like this isn't new for me too, Sonya.

You think everything is about you and your life changing. What about my life and how I feel and what I want? I'm not going to do something I don't want to do and moving in together is one of them."

"That's fine, Yusef. It was just a suggestion."

She didn't know what else to say as she held back tears. He'd made it painfully clear that he didn't want what she wanted. It was time she thought about moving on.

* * *

Over the next months, everything went by in a blur. Sonya threw herself into work while Yusef deejayed more nights at the club. They still saw each other but not as often. Sonya had decided to spend the night at Brenda's house. That morning, Kayron left for work and Brenda dropped Karen off at school and then made a quick run to Home of Chicken & Waffles to feed Sonya's growing craving for their chicken and waffles combo. Sonya sat in the living room, hungry, waiting for her to return and wondered what was taking her so long.

Meanwhile, Brenda was entering the restaurant, known for the best soul food in that part of town. As she scanned the to-go menu, she ordered the savory fried chicken, soft buttered waffles, collard greens, mac and cheese and a side of buttermilk cornbread. After paying for her meal, she walked out the door and bumped into Dray who was headed inside the restaurant.

"Hey, Brenda." He embraced her with a polite hug. "Long time, no see."

"Hi Dray, it's been a while. But I see you're fully recovered since the accident." Dray was looking sharp in a white Nike jogging suit and matching sneakers.

"Oh yeah, they can't keep a brother down for too long."

"I heard that." She smiled "Well it was good seeing you," Brenda said, trying to rush off.

"Wait. How's Sonya?"

"Sonya's fine. I better go, Dray, before my food gets cold." Brenda began to walk away before he could ask any more questions, but it was obvious that he missed Sonya.

"Do you think I should call her?" Dray called out.

Brenda hesitated; she knew he wasn't going to let her leave without an explanation as he genuinely cared about Sonya. But, right now she was going through a rough time being pregnant and dealing with Yusef's mess. The last thing Sonya needed was Dray coming back into her life. Plus, how would he feel about calling if he knew she was pregnant?

"No," Brenda said over her shoulder, "I don't think you should call her. Take care,

Dray."

* * *

Twenty minutes later, Brenda came walking through the door.

"It's about time. What did you do? Get lost in your own neighborhood?" Sonya joked.

"Hush up." Brenda handed Sonya her treasured chicken and waffles combo. I didn't get lost."

Sonya tore into the bag immediately. "Well, what happened?"

"Nothing Sonya." Brenda didn't want to bring it up that she saw Dray, but she knew Sonya wouldn't let it go. "I ran into somebody I know."

"Who was it?"

"Why?"

"I want to know." Sonya had an idea who it was since Brenda wasn't saying much. She was so enjoying her chicken combo, but just

114

had to know if she was right. Finally Sonya blurted out, "How's Dray? Did you tell him?"

Brenda paused, "He's fine and hell no! It's not my place to tell him that you're pregnant. We didn't talk long, but he did ask about you." She took a short breath. "He also wanted to know if he should call you."

Sonya raised an eyebrow. "Really, what did you say?"

"To be honest with you, I told him he shouldn't and left it at that. Now, can we talk about something else, please? And finish them mac and greens before I take them." Brenda waved the subject off.

Sonya smiled inwardly. She wouldn't admit it to Brenda, but she had secretly hoped Dray would call her. Now, she seriously doubted it.

* * *

"Hey Sonya. Baby, I miss you."

Sonya thought she was going to pass out

when she heard Dray's voice on the line. It felt so good to hear him say that.

"I miss you, too, Dray. You just don't know how much. We've always been able to work through our problems. A month without speaking at the most, but almost a year? How did we let that happen?"

"I don't know, Sonya. I guess we needed that time apart. But, I can't stand it anymore. I want to see you."

Sonya's heart fluttered but she knew she couldn't let Dray see her like this. Being pregnant was the last thing she wanted to tell him, but he had a right to know. He was a major part of her past and whether she wanted to admit it or not, she loved him.

Noting her hesitation and unusual silence, Dray asked, "Sonya, can I see you?"

"Dray, a lot has happened since we last spoke."

"Like what? I bumped into Brenda and

she said I shouldn't call you, but I called anyway. You didn't get married on me, did you?"

"No, I didn't get married, but I am pregnant."

There was an immediate pause.

"I know you weren't expecting to hear that, and I'm sorry."

"Why didn't you tell me?"

"Honestly, because I was scared."

"Scared of what?"

"Hurting you, I guess."

"It's too late for that. You just hurt me more by waiting this long to tell me. Were you ever going to tell me? Don't answer that." Dray said. "Who's the father?" He had a pretty good idea of who it was, but he wanted her to confirm it.

"It's the deejay from Club Dread," she whispered into the phone.

Dray sighed and then said, "Wow. When

117

are you due?"

"Any day now."

"Oh, okay," he said after another long pause. "Well, congratulations."

"Thanks Dray." Sonya said softly.

"Are you two still together?"

"Barely, I think we're only hanging in there because of the baby."

"I see." Dray was speechless. "I better let you go. But I'm here if you need anything. Take care of you and the baby. And Sonya, in spite of it all, it's never too late to tell you how I truly feel about you...I love you," he said quickly and ended the call before she could respond or even say goodbye.

WELCOME TO PARENTHOOD

After her call with Dray, Sonya hung up the phone and laid there on the bed in Brenda's guest room. She'd gone from hanging out in the club to having a baby. She missed having fun. While Yusef was playing records, drinking and socializing she was at home, bored, big, hungry and depressed. She couldn't believe the life changes she had experienced. What if she'd never spoken to Yusef? What if he'd never come home with her the night they met? What if she hadn't had sex with him? What if she wasn't pregnant? Too bad she thought about all the 'what ifs' after they'd happened.

She hadn't followed any of the warning signs that were given to her. When Yusef told her he was in a relationship her mind had said kick him out the car, drive away, and don't look back. Then there was when Brenda kept warning her to just be careful-it's a fun thing not a love thing. Sonya tried to find every excuse for why she shouldn't be in the situation she was in.

She didn't regret anything that happened between her and Yusef. Even though she should've known better than to get involved with a man that was on the rebound. Yusef might claim to love her, but it was easy to say when you could use it to escape the hurt and pain you were feeling from someone else. Sonya had been there to help him ease that pain. His ex-girlfriend had never left him. All she did was give him time and space to realize that there was no one that could compare to her. That's why he couldn't commit fully to her because his ex-girlfriend had every intention of getting him back.

Sonya got up from the bed to use the bathroom when her water broke. It popped like a water balloon all over the floor. In an instant panic, she yelled for Brenda and immediately reached for her cell phone to call her doctor and then Yusef.

* * *

In route to the hospital, Sonya called her parents and brother to meet her there. They were all excited to see the birth of the new addition to their family as they waited in the maternity ward waiting room.

"Dinner and a back rub, it's a girl." Brenda bet her husband.

Kayron disagreed. "No, I'll bet you dinner and full body massage, it's a boy."

"You're on!"

After three hours of labor, Sonya was exhausted but when she heard her son yell at the top of his lungs she knew it was all worth it. Yusef was standing off to the side taking photos. Sonya was lying in the hospital bed holding their new son and thinking about where life would lead them. She'd gone from enjoying life every weekend in the club to bringing a life into the world.

Yusef wanted to hold his son. "Thank you, baby," he said as he kissed her and took the newborn from her arms. Sonya's parents and Derrick hovered around him, peeking into the blanket, waiting their turn to welcome the new baby to their family.

"There's no denying that baby, Yusef. He looks just like you," Brenda said. Everyone in the room noisily agreed.

"Congratulations you two," Kayron boasted.

"Thanks," they responded in unison.

Brenda walked over to Sonya. "How do you feel?"

"Girl, don't even ask."

"Look at your parents, couldn't be

prouder of their first grandbaby. And Derrick, you'd think he was the dad, with those cigars." Sonya and Brenda laughed. "So, now what's my godson's name?" she proudly asked.

"Your godson's name is Jayson Lamar Turner."

"Ah, cute little Jayson," Brenda cooed at him.

Derrick hugged Sonya around her neck and kissed her cheek, as did their parents, who were crying, ecstatic about Jayson.

"Well, sis," Derrick said, "I'm going to take Mom and Dad home. I know you're exhausted, so we're going to go and let you get some rest. I'll be back later to get acquainted with my new nephew."

"Yeah, we're going to head out too," Brenda agreed.

"Thanks for coming," Yusef said as he shook everyone's hands.

When they stepped into the hallway, Kayron glanced over at Brenda.

"I already know what you're thinking. I owe you dinner and a full body massage."

"Yes, you do. But, I'll collect on that another day. Right now let's go pick up Karen and head home. After seeing Sonya's baby, I want to be with my family tonight."

She gazed at him lovingly, in his eyes. "I love you, Mr. Kayron Hawkins."

"I love you, too, Mrs. Brenda Hawkins."

They walked out of the hospital holding hands, which confirmed their renewed bond together.

* * *

"It's been six months since Jayson was born, what do you mean you don't have time for him?"

"Sonya, just what I said, I barely have time for myself."

"It's funny how you had all the time in the

world to have sex with me and even took me out on occasion. Now all of a sudden, you're too busy or the drive is *too* far to come over. Before we had a baby you were able to do all the things you wanted to do. How can you fix your mouth to say that about your own son?"

"I can't deal with this right now. I'm still confused, and I need time to think."

"You know what? You have been saying that same crap ever since we met. I am so tired of hearing it! Do what you want Yusef, because we don't need you."

"Sonya, it's hard to walk away from my past and I'm trying to work through my feelings."

"After all this time, you're still trying to work through your feelings? Whatever Yusef, it's over. You've made your decision on where you want to be and my son doesn't need you or the time you feel you don't have to give or to spend with him. I want you out of here."

"Sonya, don't be like this. We'll always be bonded for life."

"GET OUT!" She yelled.

Without saying another word, Yusef turned to head for the front door. Sonya was trying her hardest to hold back the tears.

The minute she slammed the door behind him, she slumped to the floor and cried her eyes out for all she had put up with. Not only was Yusef walking out on her, but she never thought he would turn and walk away from his own flesh and blood.

LIFE CHANGES

Six Months Later

Working full-time with crazy hours was a hard routine with a one-year-old, but it kept Sonya busy. She missed Jayson so much during the day while he was at daycare. But at the end of the day, when she picked him up, he made her day when he greeted her full of smiles, kisses, and baby gibberish. She enjoyed being a single mother and had a loving support system with Brenda, Derrick and her parents always available. She watched him sleep, crawl, laugh, smile, babble and reach out to give her hugs. Seeing his first tooth arrive, recording his first steps. All the treasured first in a baby's life were the most precious. She didn't care too much for the diaper changing, but she loved her son and every bit of motherhood.

She hadn't heard from Yusef but he'd made it painfully clear he was going back to his ex and that he didn't have time for his son. She didn't take him to court-like Brenda had suggested-forcing him to take care of his responsibility. She hadn't had her son to trap him. She had her son for her. She figured that eventually, Yusef's own guilt would be punishment enough for walking away from his child.

Sonya walked into her condo with her son in her arms to the smell of a nice aroma.

"Hey baby, I didn't expect you to be here. What are you doing home so early?"

"Waiting for you two. I wanted to surprise you."

Sonya glanced over at the dining room table to see that Dray had prepared a wonderful meal. He even had Jayson's highchair at the table. He grabbed her around the waist to hold them close to him while Jayson was still in her arms.

"I love you, Sonya St. Jermaine." He kissed her lips.

Jayson struggled, trying to get in on the hugs and kisses, reaching out to Dray. "Pop, Pop, Pop."

Dray had fallen in love with him the first moment they met and had become a loving father to Jayson.

"Hey little man, your pop loves you, too," Dray said, referring to himself. Dray reached out his arms and took Jayson away from Sonya. He hugged him close and kissed him, then strapped him in his highchair, giving him a wafer and something to play with.

Dray and Sonya had reconnected a few months prior when he was fighting a house fire and she and her camera crew had reported on the scene. They were happy to see each other. Once things were under control, they decided to get together and play catch up.

Dray was surprised to learn she and Yusef weren't together and that he had walked away from his son. They were able to clear the air about a lot of things and their relationship fell right back into their usual friends and lovers categories, minus the being enemies part.

She smiled over at him, "We love you, too, Dray McKinnis. This is a really nice surprise." Sonya walked over to sit down at the dining room table.

"Is this champagne on the table?"

"Yes, I thought we could toast to our getting married."

"What did you just say?" Sonya said, stunned.

"Sonya, I'm very happy living with you and loving you. And, I remember when I was in the hospital that day and you said you couldn't imagine losing me. Well, I can't imagine life without you and now Jayson, either."

Dray handed her the champagne glass and she noticed the sparkling diamond floating at the bottom.

Dray got down on his knee and asked, "Sonya, will you marry me?"

"Yes, Dray I'll marry you," she answered as she began to cry. She'd always thought this moment would be with her son's father. But she learned a valuable lesson when she was with Yusef, which was it's never too late to return to a past love. Who would've thought she and Jayson would be bonded for life with Dray McKinnis?

Thank you for reading.
Here's a sneak peek at book four...

What Could've Been
(Renee and Bradsen's story)
TIME WILL TELL

"Bradsen, what are we doing here?" Renee wanted to know. They were aboard Bradsen's luxury yacht. Renee hadn't been on it since Bradsen broke the news to her about Kayron still being alive.

"I brought you here so we could talk, and I also have something for you."

Bradsen handed her an envelope. Renee remembered the last time Bradsen had something for her at that same spot on the sun deck, it wasn't good news. She didn't want to relive the old memories. *What could it be this time?* she thought.

Renee hesitated to take the envelope from him, but Bradsen urged her on. She pulled out the contents and read it silently to herself.

"Are you serious?" Renee's eyes got wide. "You really want to do this?"

"Yes, I love you Renee and I think it's time for us to take the next step in our relationship."

She continued to stare at the papers in disbelief until Bradsen got down on bended knee and asked, "Renee Lawson, will you go away with me?"

"Very funny, Bradsen Myers, of course I'll go to Italy with you."

He stood to kiss her, "One day I'll be back down on my knee, but only when you're ready."

"Okay, well, when do we leave?" Renee was excited. She had never been to Italy before.

"How about now? We'll dock at the nearest port and leave from there."

"Now? But what about our clothes, letting

our families know..." Renee started to ramble.

"Relax baby," Bradsen reassured her. "Everything has been taken care of and we'll tell everyone about our trip in the next book," he joked as they sailed away.

To be continued...

"Meet the Author"
Tesa Erven

Tesa Erven was born and raised in San Francisco, California. She currently resides in New Jersey with her husband and two children. She works as an office administrator for a global outplacement firm. In her spare time, she enjoys reading, writing and singing. She released her first published work, The Loose End, in 2015. You can visit her website at www.tesaerven.com or connect with her on Facebook at www.facebook.com/authortesaerven.

Made in the USA
Charleston, SC
07 February 2017